This book belongs to:

_____

Fun in Vista Village

Barbara Anderson

illustrated by **Ambreen Siddiqui**

Text copyright © 2019 Barbara Anderson. All rights reserved.
Illustrations copyright © 2019 Ambreen Siddiqui. All rights reserved.

For Keith, who always lets me be me, and Jayson, who has always been himself.

Hi. I'm Terry Turtle.

I like to play baseball, but when I run, my shell is too heavy.

Sooo...

This is my friend Katie Kangaroo.

She's different from other kangaroos.

Instead of hopping like this...

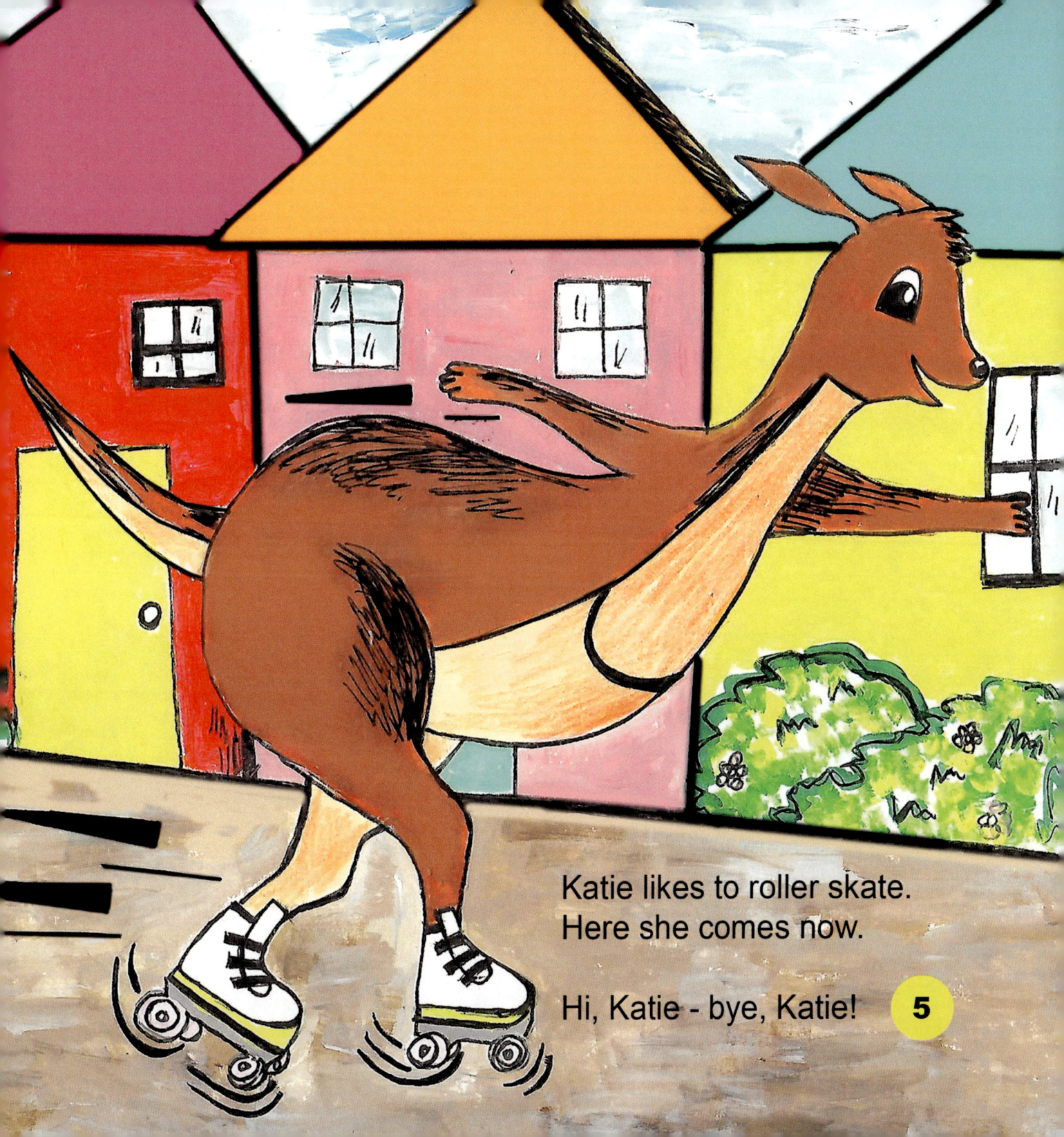

Katie likes to roller skate.
Here she comes now.

Hi, Katie - bye, Katie!

Next, meet my friend Jason Jackrabbit.

You probably know that jackrabbits usually hop like this.

Not Jason! He's different!

He uses his ears as propellers and flies where he wants to go.

Happy landing, Jason!

Now you are going to meet Danny Dove.

Of course, most doves fly wherever they go, like this...

But Danny is different!

He wears sneakers and runs all over the place.

Fast, too!

I see Amber Ant coming now.

Ants build cities in the dirt by carrying soil in their mouths.

Next we'll visit Holly Horse.

You know horses wear hard shoes that make noise when they walk.

Holly is different.

She likes to walk quietly - so she wears fuzzy slippers at home.

My last friend is Karly Kitten.

Cats and kittens don't like to get wet.

But Karly is different.

She takes a bath in her bathtub every night!

Splish, splash, Karly!

I hope you enjoyed meeting my friends and me. We are all a little different from other animals like us. We are also a lot different from each other. But we are all great friends. We know that it's okay to be different.

The best thing to be is...**YOURSELF!!!**

LET'S PLAY AGAIN SOON!!!

BYE!!!

You can be yourself, too.
Use these pages to draw and color
something about YOU!

You can be yourself, too.
Use these pages to draw and color
something about YOU!

You can be yourself, too.
Use these pages to draw and color
something about YOU!

Made in United States
Orlando, FL
08 April 2022